the
awakening of
ADAM

THE WHISTLE-PIG JOURNEYS

the *awakening of* ADAM

RON L. KUNTZ

TATE PUBLISHING & *Enterprises*

Published by Tate Publishing & Enterprises, LLC
127 E. Trade Center Terrace | Mustang, Oklahoma 73064 USA
1.888.361.9473 | www.tatepublishing.com

Tate Publishing is committed to excellence in the publishing industry. The company reflects the philosophy established by the founders, based on Psalm 68:11,
"The Lord gave the word and great was the company of those who published it."

Book design copyright © 2011 by Tate Publishing, LLC. All rights reserved.
Cover design by Joel Uber
Interior design by Nathan Harmony

Published in the United States of America

ISBN: 978-1-61777-540-6
1. Fiction: Christian: Classic & Allegory
2. Fiction: Literary
11.05.05

Dedication

My journey was made easier and far more enjoyable because of a teacher named Miss Gail Lance. To her I was, I am, and I will be eternally grateful. It is to her that I dedicate this story.

Preface

ALL OF US, IN OUR FINITE TIME ON THIS MARVELOUS planet, are on a journey. Some know where their destination will be, and some have no clue. Some have always known, and some will never know until they arrive.

As you read this story, it will become a part of your journey. For some it will become an exceedingly small part, and perhaps for a select few, it may become a memorable part. Everybody and everything that you encounter in your life will become a part of you and the journey that you are on. They all have an effect on you, and remember, you also will have an effect on them. Do well to make their way easier and more memorable!

Have a nice trip!

Alpha

I SHALL TELL YOU A STORY—IT IS THE TALE OF A JOURNEY.

On a morning in late March, something quite miraculous happened. But wait! This is a story that has to do with the animal kingdom and denotes physical attributes. Therefore, I will try to tell my story in some of the terms the animals would better relate to. They have no calendars, and therefore the term *March* has no meaning to them. So I shall try to express this tale in terms the characters themselves would better identify with. I shall begin again.

On the onset of the light, in the beginning of the plenty period, something quite miraculous happened. Although this had happened millions of times before, actually billions and billions of times before, it was still quite miraculous. In its own way it was quite unique, as it is every time it happens. A female was giving birth. The hour and even the day have little, if any, meaning, for this event was happening deep in the earth where light does not penetrate and day and night do not exist. There was only the darkness.

When the birthing was complete, there were four tiny, helpless, very naked babies and one very exhausted mother. Though totally spent, she still found the energy to lick them clean and then huddle them together beneath her. They instinctively found the nourishment that she provided. This was a family of the Chisel Tooth Tribe. The Chisel Tooth Tribe is composed of many clans. There is the Squeaky Clan, the Flat Tail Clan, and the Tree Clan, to name a few. This family belonged to the Whistle-pig Clan.

All births are unique because never before have the same young existed. Now, it seems as if all newly born whistle-pigs are the same, as they all surely look like their ancestors did at birth for thousands and thousands of years. But each is, and always has been, different in its own special way. This litter consisted of entities that had never before existed and would never exist again. Yes, each was special! This litter, however, was even more special than any that had ever existed before. A gift never before given had been granted to one of these lowly, tunnel-dwelling whistle-pigs—at least as far as we know! How was he different? That is for you to decide. Why was he special? That is not for me to say. Suffice it to say that he was indeed a very different little whistle-pig!

This is his story. My next problem is that whistle-pigs have no names. They recognize each other by their smell. This is a far better way than a name. If we call a human baby *Sam*, are there not many who will also have this name? As he grows older his appearance will change, and

Ron L. Kuntz

there may be others who will look similar. A scent, however, will always be the same. This mother whistle-pig will always know her young. The scent of each had already been imprinted in her memory, never to be forgotten or changed. Each scent is, and always will be, unique.

Here I again encounter a problem in the telling of my tale. I cannot describe subtle variances of odors, nor do I possess the ability to distinguish them. For the purpose of practicality, I shall give him a name. A foreign and artificial thing this is, for the clan has no use for such things. But I do! I shall call him Adam, and this is the story of his finite time on this planet.

As Adam firmly grasped his mother's teat in his mouth, he was aware that the milk was warm and good, and he vaguely knew that it was good for him. His sister and two brothers were also greedily drinking, but theirs was purely an instinctive behavior. Adam's actions were mostly instinctive—but not totally.

After drinking his fill, he felt drowsy, so he began to go to sleep. He felt happy, content, and safe in a newborn, helpless way. Now, it is a fact that whistle-pigs cannot smile. It is anatomically impossible for one to do so. But one should remember that a genuine, true smile comes from the heart and the soul, not from the lips and jowls. As he slept, Adam had a trace of the tiniest of grins on his tiny, hairless face. All was right with his world!

Adam's life had begun. It mainly consisted of eating, sleeping, and cuddling for warmth and affection. He became aware that there were others present besides his mother. He could not count how many, but he knew that

there were others who were competition for food and attention. They were irksome when they trampled upon him,
but he knew that he also did his fair share of pushing and
nudging and trampling. This gave him a faint good feeling.
The other three instinctively pushed and shoved for their
food. Adam did it with gusto, and strangely, developed a
feeling of respect for his siblings. Not love, but respect.

On the surface, the times of light and the times of dark
passed. The only meaning of this in an underground system of tunnels is the passage of time. The four gained
weight and size and fur. Their eyes had opened, but in the
darkness they still could not see. They did not know the
light. All took a strange delight in pushing and wrestling
with each other. A bond was rapidly developing between
the four. It was not a bond of love, but it was indeed a
bond of affection and recognition.

Their mother would leave the den to go out and forage for bark or any greenery that could be found during
the beginning of the plenty period. Her young had needs,
and somehow she knew that she must be a good mother.
Even if they slept when she left, the four knew when she
was gone. They could not see, but they knew there was
no great, massive body to bump into and cuddle against.
They knew the others were there. They could feel the
body contact, and each of the other scents was different
and becoming imprinted into their own minds. Their eyes
could not see, but they could see through other means.

The young are one of the greatest joys of a parent.
Unfortunately, they can also be one of life's greatest thorns.
This brood was no different, except for one who was of a

Ron L. Kuntz

temperament to test the most caring mother. Yes, it was Adam. He was active! He was curious! He was indeed a pain in the tail to his mother. He would not lie still and was becoming quite a pawful!

Adam awoke one light and was aware that something was missing. There was no mother scent. He could smell the other three and could hear their soft, rhythmic breathing. Where did the mother scent go? A question that he felt needed to be finally answered! So he stumbled along the dark tunnel till the tunnel split and there were two ways to go. Which path should he take? The answer was easy! One had much more mother scent and also a strange and wonderful mixture of new scents that his twitching little nose had never experienced. They made the little body quiver with excitement and curiosity. This one had to be the one!

Now, it was strange how hard it was for his new legs to keep going. This was his first experience of going uphill. Gravity had never been experienced in this way. The tiny legs became tired and weary. He wanted to stop. Then a wondrous thing happened! To his brain came the sensation of light. His eyes had a use! It was a marvelous sensation. The light energized his total existence. It seemed very far off and dim but became brighter and brighter as he moved his tiny, weak legs as fast as he could. He was not afraid of this light but was drawn to it. He pushed ever upward. Something inside of him yearned for it. There was a flurry of motion as he almost reached the top. It was a blurred motion to his untrained eyes. The motion touched his nose! The motion was quivering and wet and was extremely strong with mother scent!

He had seen his mother! It was only for a second or two, and then he was being pushed and shoved back to the birth chamber. The words *gently nudged* did not apply! Mother was not impressed and surely not amused by his adventure. But he had seen his mother. She was no longer just mother scent and a warm sensation. It was wondrous!

Adam was made very aware of her displeasure. His tiny feet could not match his mother's, and his size and strength were even more pathetic as he rolled down the entrance to the division. He actually rolled quite well! Even on the flat part, she continued to roll him back to the birth chamber. As he rolled, he heard murmurings deep in the throat of Mother. It was a non-PG-rated dialect used by mother clan members for countless generations when about to kick their young's ungrateful little tails. For countless generations it was a bluff, and for countless generations the offspring knew that it was a bluff!

The other three were rudely awakened as he slammed into them. Fortunately, they had not yet acquired an adult vocabulary, but they were now definitely in poor humor. Before they had decided on a suitable punishment for their errant little brother, they noticed the mother scent and knew that breakfast was about to be served. All four grabbed on and greedily drank all they could. Transgressions were quickly forgotten!

As he suckled, Adam wanted to tell the others of the marvel he had discovered. But how? How could he tell them of something that he did not understand? And how could they understand? These were his thoughts as the warm milk filled his stomach and blurred the excitement that he had just experienced. He was now very sleepy indeed. Adam's stomach was filled with milk, but his mind was filled even more with wonder.

Adam was awed.

Education

ADAM'S ADVENTURE WAS A WAKEUP CALL FOR MOTHER. Her young had a growing appetite, and her milk supply was growing shorter each day. The brood had to be taken out of the safety of the den and introduced to other foods. She did not totally understand why, but she was hesitant on doing this. There were dangers, but it had to be done!

Very early the next light, Mother left as usual, only this time she returned in a short period. She had done her recon. It was safe, at least for the moment. She cooed and chortled and pushed and prodded them down the tunnel. Adam needed no prodding! He knew where she wanted them to go. His tiny legs easily got him ahead of his mother, and he was on his way. Mother was so busy with the other three that she never missed him. Or perhaps she was aware but knew he that could not be stopped.

There was now no hesitation where the tunnel forked. There it was! It was faint and very soft and seemed so very far away. It was a goal. He would reach the light with its wonders. This time gravity was not much of a match. Another day's growth and great excitement had leveled the playing field for the little one. His tiny legs moved as fast as they could, and his goal got closer and closer. As the light became stronger, the black, beady, little eyes adjusted fairly well—until he got to the top.

It was so bright! He blinked and blinked, and with each blink, images began to form. He did not dare to shut his eyes now, for he feared it would all disappear as if in a dream. It was so big, and there was so much wonderment! He did not know what he saw, but he greedily drank with his eyes as he had drunk when being fed. He did not understand why he thought this, but somehow he knew that he should go no farther. He wanted to run and smell everything, and somehow he thought to perhaps taste these things. Instinct prevailed, and he stayed at the burrow opening and only explored with his eyes. He became aware of an object partially hidden by the shrubs. For a second he looked and immediately shut his eyes tightly. It was the shiny orb. Although still very low in the sky and partially veiled by leaves, it was very bright for tiny eyes. *How did it hurt me? It did not touch me*, he thought. A puzzlement! The first of many for the little adventurer.

Adam's thoughts were broken by the arrival of Mother and the other three. They needed no prodding now. Curiosity is a strong motivator! The three also blinked as their eyes adjusted to this newly found world. With Mother for protection, the four began their exploration. With extended necks and wary noses, they sniffed everything. If it smelled good, it went into their mouths. With a violent shaking of the head, some was spit out, and some was chewed slowly and sometimes cautiously swallowed. Imitation and exploration was the learning method. The education process had truly begun.

So it was each day; Mother would give less and less nourishment and finally none. She began to push her babies gently away with her wet, wiggling nose, and if they persisted, the pushing became less gentle. If they would not accept this and still persisted, a stinging nip always worked. Food must be found in this wonderful, lighted world. So each day they ventured farther and farther away, not only from their den, but also from their mother. The little noses worked with a passion, eagerly memorizing the scents of the plants that were to be their food for the remainder of their lives. It was a far better process than always letting the tongue decide.

Food was not the only reason for venturing farther and farther away. It was curiosity. The thrill of exploration and discovery was irresistible. There was a strong inner need to keep safely close to their den, but the clan seemed to have burrows everywhere. Each den had more than one entrance, and there were shallow holes only dug for the possibility of a quick escape. The Whistle-pig Clan had a love for digging. Something the young needed to know was that escape seemed close and everywhere, except per-haps when they would need it the most! In play and for real, their senses were being honed to a fine point. They were quick to scurry home or to a neighbor's den when the danger alarm was raised by an adult. If not heeded, a none-too-gentle nip in the tail region was administered by their ever-vigilant mother.

As each light passed, their knowledge increased. Some of this knowledge was social, and some was survival. Seeing some of the adults sitting upright on their haunches with noses raised high into the breeze seemed to be a behavior to be emulated. For the clumsy pups, it was indeed a challenge. This was especially true on the hillside. Many a time Adam would give a squeal as he fell and rolled partially down the hillside, only to scamper back and try again. After mastering this, the next step was the whistle. Now, this is a skill that is not often used but can be very useful. The small clans, where the great orb disappears, use it much more often. Anyway, Adam thought that it would be great to sit on the entrance mound and give this shrill one note for all to hear. Did you ever try to teach a child to whistle through their teeth? The whistle was a skill Adam was not yet ready for.

Tail language was another necessary skill. Yes, I said tail language! Since most people do not have one, it may seem pretty unnecessary. To a whistle-pig, it was used a lot and was necessary to learn. Almost every emotion had its own particular movement of that short little tail. It was used for danger, excitement, bluffing, and even romance. Although we often ignore the importance of this language, Adam did not. Adam became fluent in tail!

It was a pleasant phase in their lives. As their education progressed, Mother began to pay less and less attention to their antics and even to their safety. They were now almost one-third grown and were being given adult status.

Life begins early in the animal kingdom. Their world had become a place to learn. Lessons must be learned quickly and well, for the world can be a most unforgiving arena. Of the four, Adam knew and understood that the best.

Adam was a very good student!

Sister

As he cautiously emerged into the warming rays of the rising, shiny orb, Adam used all of his newly acquired skills. Before poking his vulnerable head above the entrance plane, he would pause and view everything above him. The ever-twitching nose would inhale all of the aromas and scents that drifted by. Scent is a valuable tool in a whistle-pig's defensive system. It is far more than a tool used for recognition or to enjoy the blooming vegetation. If no danger was signaled by the olfactory, Adam's ears would perk up and scan in all directions. He would hear the Winged Tribe. The singing of the small clans was a good sign. The harsh, rapid call of the Large Noisy Clan was a sign of danger. He listened for any rustling of the grasses and leaves that was not a normal occurrence. He listened especially for sounds that were methodical and were moving. Ears are also a major weapon of defense in a whistle-pig's life, even though they appear small. When all was deemed safe, Adam's head would slowly emerge. A whistle-pig's eyes are truly some of the best in the animal kingdom, but there is a flaw! Color cannot be detected. The eyes are superb in darkness or at spotting motion, even at great distances. Everything appears in the brain as white, black, and varying shades of gray. If a hungry predator does not move and is downwind, the eyes are a very poor, if not dangerous, source of information.

As Adam stood on the dirt mound at the entrance, he saw no cause for alarm. Suddenly, out of the tunnel scampered his sister and two brothers. They almost knocked him over in their haste for breakfast.

Adam desperately wanted to tell them of the error of their ways. He would dearly have loved to be able to tell them the thoughts that went through his mind and listen to what they would tell him. They could only understand the simple one-thought grunts and chortles and purrs that were used in everyday life. The occasional whistle through the large front teeth had small meaning to them. Because Adam did not always follow routine clan behavior, his siblings and others of his group were instinctively beginning to view him with suspicion, and perhaps some fear. Adam was different!

A wild thought raced through his mind. What if he gave the alarm? The three would scamper over him to the safety of the den. There they would cower and wait and have their breakfast delayed while he gorged on what he wanted. The thought amused him greatly! Now, it is an absolute fact that normal whistle-pigs cannot laugh, nor are they able to comprehend a joke. There is no sense of humor in this clan. But Adam chuckled gleefully as he pictured the result of that prank. The three would emerge

Ron L. Kuntz

later and not even know they had been the object of his humor. Then he thought of his group. They also would heed his warning. They also would be inconvenienced but never suspect his treachery. Yes, it would be treachery. Members of the Chisel Tooth Tribe never question the danger alarm. They instinctively obey it. That is the way it should be! Adam ceased his mirth and now felt small and ashamed. This time he was glad that none of his clan could understand his thoughts.

He began his breakfast. His coordination had vastly improved, and he could now easily stand on his haunches, braced by the stout little tail, to pluck off only the tenderest of the clover blossoms and the youngest of the new shoots. As his mouth feasted, so did his other senses.

His eyes took in the swaying of the grasses and the quivering of the leaves. It was a ballet of nature, there for the watching. Even though Adam did not know what a ballet was, he watched the show that was being provided.

His ears listened to the wind that produced the swaying, dancing plants. He listened for the small-winged clans. He loved to hear their wonderful songs. Each clan had its own song. They were not singing now, and he was sad that they were not providing his breakfast with their symphony.

The perpetually moving nose was providing its own symphony of aromas. He loved the flowering plants. He loved them with both his nose and his mouth! He smelled the dirt from the freshly dug burrows. His was a clan that constantly dug burrows. Sometimes he wondered if this digging was a nervous habit, or for added safety, or if his clan just loved the smell of fresh dirt. He could smell the water from the little brook that ran at the base of the hill. But wait! Suddenly, to his active little nose, there came a new scent. It was not one that he had ever smelled before.

His insatiable curiosity began to turn to a feeling of uneasiness and perhaps dread. He did not know why this change was happening. The scent grew stronger, and with it, a strange sense of danger. He stood up as high as his back toes would allow, and his now stiff little tail began to twitch. He saw his two brothers and his sister. They had strayed farther away than they usually did. They seemed fine, and there was no danger to be seen.

Adam's eyes suddenly saw movement. With the movement, a shape could be defined. It was much bigger than a mature whistle-pig and had large, sharp ears, which had started to twitch. A front paw was now being nervously raised.

What Adam saw was a member of the Sharp Nose Tribe. There were two clans. To Adam, they would be the Dark Gray Clan and the Light Gray Clan. For the sake of narration, and because I am a member of the Two Legged Tribe, I will simply call them the Gray Clan and the Red Clan, for that is what they truly are. They do not know these names, for they also can only see gray. Only the Winged Tribe and the Two Legged Tribe are able to see them as the Red and Gray Clans.

What Adam saw was a female of the Red Clan. Adam sounded the danger alarm. Without question or hesitation, all members of the group, including Mother, heeded this call and scampered for the nearest burrow to safety. The three siblings started their race for safety, but they

Ron L. Kuntz

had ventured far. There is no chivalry in fear and panic. The two males, who had already grown larger than their sister, left her behind in their mad dash for safety.

Adam watched in both horror and fascination as the red one closed the distance. She was so fast and graceful! There was no time for Adam to react. Her bushy tail, acting as an aiming rudder, stood straight out. She came from behind and clenched the fleeing little female in her teeth. It was a precise placement, as the teeth came together on the nape of the neck directly below the head. Adam watched in awe of the sureness and deftness of this move as his brothers ran past him to their safety. The scream of surprise and then pain was heard as the red one secured her grip and turned to flee. The anguished cry was quickly followed by a crunching noise and then the sister's expelled last breath through her clenched teeth.

The red one readjusted her grip, lifted her prey high, and pranced back into the brush. If only Adam could be that agile! Then he had a moment of shame at that thought. Although there was no love involved, sorrow welled up for one he had become so very accustomed to. He vowed always to remember what he had seen and heard this light. Little did he know that he could never forget.

Now that nature's drama and the danger were over, sensibility returned. Adam turned and scurried into his burrow. The images had been deeply etched onto his mind. Sometimes education comes at a high price. The scent of this red one was ingrained forever, and he vowed it would never be forgotten or forgiven! The entire group ventured out no more during this light. For Adam, an elusive and then troubled sleep was his only activity.

The next light found Adam with a very sad and troubled mind. Why had this happened? He had no real attachment for his sister, but there had been a definite bond. His brothers had left for breakfast. They were much more cautious and exhibited an amount of wariness that equaled their nervousness. While all others avoided the site, Adam went to the scene of this injustice and, with a slowly twitching nose, inhaled all the memories he could. He reinforced the last scent of his sister. To the others of the group, she would be forgotten in a few lights. To them she never would have existed. Adam deeply inhaled and stored all that could be had of the attacker. It also was now deeply etched.

He somehow knew that his sister had gone on the great departure. Where had she gone? A puzzlement! She was no longer here, but she must be somewhere! The rest of the family and group knew only that one of their number was missing, and even that would soon be gone. For the brothers, and especially for Adam, it was a stark lesson of life and survival. Adam would often think of the happenings of that light.

It was not many lights before the three brothers were forced from their home. Mother had other thoughts now, and the three were already weaned. They were forced from the security they had always known and physically driven away. Adam decided it had become quite crowded and his brothers were not the best of company. Adam was ready!

So Adam was now finally on his own. He chose what he thought was a good site far enough away and began to dig. There was no trouble (except if a large rock was rude enough to interfere) for him to dig out his new place of residence. He became the builder and the architect. It was an instinct, but Adam's home was a little different than the others.

Every dark, before sleep would overtake him, Adam relived his sister's departure.

Adam was angry.

First Great Sleep

ADAM WAS VERY COMFORTABLE IN HIS NEW HOME. IT was designed to his liking and was lined much thicker with grasses and leaves than most. It was now near the end of the cooling period. Adam was aware that the duration of the light was becoming less and less with each of the passing lights. With each new light the shadows deepened, and soon it seemed as if the shiny orb was ready to touch the ground. It was so low in the sky! It had also lost much of its warming power. Was the shiny orb going on its great departure?

Now Adam could bask in the meager warmth and not become overheated and begin to pant and finally need to go to the brook for a cooling drink. Basking was now a luxury since not much time could be given to that pleasantry. The time of the light was short, and he spent most of it eating.

Ron L. Kuntz

And eat he did! No plant in the vicinity of the den was safe. If it wasn't tasty, he clipped it at the roots and carried it back to his underground lair. He really did not understand why, but he was driven to line the sleep chamber and to eat beyond feeling full. As for the sleep chamber, it became more and more comfortable to lie in its softness, and it brought back memories of his birth den. His den smelled much better though! As he curled up for his sleep, his last thoughts were of his mother and brothers, and especially of his sister. It was a pleasant way to drift off to slumber, and often these images continued into his dreams.

As the light grew still shorter, the shadows grew longer, and Adam grew fatter—and fatter. Now, it is a fact that whistle-pigs waddle. From the oldest to the pups taking their first steps, they waddle! It seems the widespread, short, muscular legs are ideally suited not only for digging but were born to waddle. If the animal kingdom had Olympic Games and the waddle was one of the events, then Adam would indeed have had the gold around his fat little neck!

Although not quite yet grown, Adam was already about as big as any of his clan ever got. This definitely included width! He was also very furry, and his coat was not only full but shiny and sleek. In fact, one could say that he was a very handsome critter—for a large Chisel Tooth!

The lights were getting even colder. The thick layer of fat provided superb insulation against the bitter winds. Although the shiny orb had lost almost all of its power to warm, Adam was actually very comfortable. The leaves changed to different shades of gray and then began to fall from their lofty perches. Adam loved to watch them as they floated and swirled to the ground. What a wonderful thing to happen! Adam was amused as he pictured himself floating in the breeze. He smiled as he thought, in his present condition, what type of breeze it would take for him to gently waft in the air.

He began to have strong urges to go down to his cozy lair and nap. This seemed silly with the light now being so precious. He fought these urges with all his might, but they continued to grow. Many times during the waking hours, his face erupted into a huge yawn, showing the large teeth and a large, gaping mouth. Not what one would expect from such a tiny snout! A full-body stretch always followed.

On one emergence from his shelter, a curious thing was observed. It was almost mid-light, and there were none of the group to be seen. He also had not smelled or heard anyone during his security exit. Strange! Mid-light and he was the first!

He waddled listlessly down to the brook to get his first drink. The water was gone! In its place was a shiny, light gray substance. The brook was no longer a liquid! It had turned to a solid. But wait! Adam cocked his head to the side and could still hear the water. It seemed to be trapped under this strange coating. He put his right paw on this strange substance. It was no match for his superb mass. There was a sharp crack, and the paw dropped into the water. Adam recoiled in surprise but immediately began an investigation. The eyes detected nothing of danger, and the ever-twitching nose detected nothing. It only smelled

Ron L. Kuntz

water. So a slightly confused Adam drank his fill and then began the trip up the hill.

With his longing for sleep had also come a loss of energy and enthusiasm. Lethargy had set in. The distance from the brook had gotten greater! Upon arriving at his earthen doorstep, a massive, full-body stretch was in order, followed by a toothy, gaping yawn. *Perhaps a short nap would also be in order*, he thought.

He began to go into the entrance and suddenly stopped. He backed out and took a long, three hundred sixty-degree look at his world. Why? He did not know. He was too tired to care why. Three feet into the downward journey he stopped and did another strange thing. He began to dig the tunnel wider. The front paws gouged out dirt and rocks from the floor and sides. This was pushed backward to the powerful back legs. They in turn threw the material into a mound that effectively sealed the entrance with only a glimmer of light at the top. Puzzled, he looked at what he had just done. Why had he done this? Why would you close out the light? He did not know anything except that he was tired and very, very sleepy. Besides, after his short nap, it would be quite easy to remove this barricade to the outside.

There was one long, wistful look at the tiny light at the top of his creation. A short waddle and he was in the luxury of the well-lined sleep chamber. Then he curled into a tight ball, with the bushy tail covering a surprisingly docile little nose. There were pleasant thoughts of his short day—except for the trip back up the hill! Now for a short nap to regain his strength. So tired and content was he that he barely noticed his heartbeat begin to decrease and his curious little brain begin to shut down. His thoughts dissipated into the vast expanse of eternity, as had those of countless of his clan since their creation. A realm was being entered where there were no thoughts, no choices, no dreams, and no memories. It was a realm of eternity and peace.

The sleep period had begun.

Adam was unaware.

Ron L. Kuntz

The First Awakening

It was a little more than halfway into the sleep period. If you could get by the earthen plug that had been thrown across the tunnel, and if your eyes became accustomed to the light coming through the tiny air hole on the top of this predator and temperature barrier, you could make out the subject of our tale. Actually, I hope you brought a flashlight, because far from the barrier is the sleep chamber, and it is in total darkness. It was the perfect floor plan for a tomb. Adam was still curled into a tight ball, and at first you would assume a tomb was the proper place for him. He had not, however, experienced his great departure. Instead, it was the beginning of his earthly rebirth.

The heart of this lowly mammal began to beat faster. Very slowly at first, to be sure; soon it would be up to ten, maybe twelve beats a minute. If you watched long enough, you would see a breath being drawn. The awakening would be gradual and take hours. As the increased blood and oxygen coursed through his brain, thoughts began to evolve. He began to dream!

He dreamed of his first cycle. All of his dreams were of the pleasant variety. He especially formed images of his first experience of turning the corner from the birthing den and seeing the soft glow of the light. It had opened up a new life and existence for him, full of wonderful things. Some of these things puzzled him, but to Adam, that increased their wonderment!

Adam's body temperature, which had hovered slightly above freezing, was increasing and beginning to approach normal. His eyes began to flutter as the sleep period dissipated. As he gained a conscious state, the little, black, beady eyes saw nothing. There was confusion at first. He did not know where he was or why he was there. A better-functioning brain and instinct overcame these questions, and he knew he must follow the slightly scented current of air that came from above. His muscles complained slightly as he staggered to the barrier. The complaining of the unused muscles would increase with each future great sleep; however, the enthusiasm and excitement to reach the light above would more than compensate for the aging muscles and joints.

Arriving at his barrier to the outside, he began to paw at the semi-frozen earth. His paws began to dig with more and more haste, and soon the muscular arms, although weakened, had cleared a small passage, through which he squeezed.

Ron L. Kuntz

His eyes blinked as they became accustomed to this wonderful stimulus. But wait! He could not just rush outward into what he had waited for and so craved. For what seemed like an eternity, he waited. He sniffed. The air was cold, and there was little of interest in it. It was quite sterile. He listened. There were no songs or rustlings, only wind noises. Only after he had satisfied those stages of the survival instinct did he slowly raise his head and look.

What a sight he beheld! He could see through all the trees and shrubs. It would be hard for an enemy to hide there. The entire landscape was a collage of gray, except there were patches on the ground that were of a shade he had never seen before except at mid-light high in the sky. Do clouds fall from the sky during the sleep period? The white was dazzling! It shone and sparkled so brightly when the rays of the shiny orb fell upon it. What would it sparkle and shine like if the orb were high above as in the hot period? The orb was low, and he saw all the shadows were as long as they were when the dark approached.

Now, all whistle-pigs are curious, but they are cautiously curious. Once they have satisfied their curiosity, they quickly move on. Not Adam! He reveled in his curiosity! Every new experience was a wonder. Life itself was a wonder! He had such an urge to explore and to explore quickly.

He rushed to the nearest of the sparkling, white patches. The tiny, dark brown nose wiggled and sniffed and wiggled some more, but no scent was to be had. The curiosity was now even greater. He sniffed so hard that his nose touched the glistening mass. It was soft. It was cold! His head jerked back at this. Had he been bitten? Or had this material nuzzled him? His nose felt fine now, so he had not been bitten. The exploring nose sniffed all the harder and touched it again. It actually felt good! So the nose went farther and farther in until his face was fully into it.

When Adam pulled back, some of this new material was clinging to his nose and fur and especially his long whiskers. The beady little bug eyes crossed as they watched the dab of white on his nose disappear into a droplet of liquid. He shook his head, and sparkles flew everywhere! His tongue went to clean off his face, and he was startled. It was water! Very cold water to be sure, but definitely water. It was like the brook before the sleep period began.

He put some into his mouth. What a sensation! It tickled and stimulated, and he could feel it disappear on his tongue. Stuffing his mouth, he chewed. He did not realize how much time had passed since he began his sleep. He did know he was thirsty and ate his fill. Now, he realized this short nap had also made him hungry, and he looked for something to fill his empty belly. The water had awakened his stomach. There were no tender grasses or leaves, but there was bark on the shrubs, and the dried grasses smelled acceptable.

As he turned to satisfy this hunger, an urge overtook the basic needs. Running into his new discovery, he rolled in it. He plowed a path with his nose, and of course the little paws dug into it. The front paws furiously moved the cold, soft mass to the hind legs, which sprayed it into a plume behind him.

Now, fully-grown whistle-pigs do not play. They are of a very serious nature. Frolic is not a word in their very

Ron L. Kuntz

limited vocabulary. But Adam frolicked! Others had also emerged and watched in amazement. Had Adam gone completely mad? Was he hurt? Was this the first step for his great departure? Then it came to them. It was only Adam! They continued on their business and tried to avoid the flying crystals.

The complaining belly did not like this frolic business and gave reminders that there was something that was much more essential. Ever so reluctantly, Adam waddled to the dried grasses and shrubbery and began to munch. It was delicious! In the plenty period, this stuff would not be touched. It is amazing how even a gourmet chef will readily devour anything if hungry enough. So Adam satisfied his noisy little belly, and since it had shrunken, it was quickly stuffed.

With a full and content belly, a desire to sleep had again become overpowering. The front paws were extended to their limit; a gaping yawn revealed his glistening (albeit slightly yellow), huge, front teeth. A short nap definitely seemed in order. He quickly waddled to the burrow and lumbered down. He then sealed the entrance before he knew that he had done it. That was silly! When his little nap was over, it would have to be opened again.

Adam's short nap became a little longer than he imagined. The sleep period was not yet completed.

It would be forty-two lights before the awakening process would begin all over again. As Adam's heart rate again decreased and his body temperature again dropped to near freezing, Adam frolicked!

Day to Day

AS THE CYCLE OF PERIODS PASSED, ADAM GREW TO A SIZE that even the largest of the males respected. They were not capable of envy. He had differences that his group could not comprehend; therefore, he was held in suspicion as an outsider and shunned. He was respected, to be sure. He was the one who first gave a danger warning to the group. The males knew that he was quite a formidable opponent in their jockeying for supremacy. The Whistle-pig Clan was big into bluffing. Adam did not play that game! In combat, Adam did not react to their aggressive moves as tradition dictated. Adam cheated! But what is cheating? Could it not be considered simply a way to improve a game by changing a rule or even adding a new one? He did not react to their moves. He anticipated them and always struck first. He knew where to inflict the most pain and still not cause any permanent injury. Injuries, no matter how slight they may appear, are always serious in the animal arena. A blow to the ego is usually quite adequate to the Whistle-pig Clan. He became a force to be avoided. He was respected! He did not seek or desire it. It came.

Adam never mated. No other male dared to challenge him, but there was no kinship or attachment to any of the females. He was no threat to any of the other males in that regard, or in any regard! Are the other tribes and clans afraid of others who are different and whom they do not understand?

Adam lived a solitary existence.

At dawn his routine would begin by wandering out of his burrow and nibbling, if not gorging, on the plenty of his little valley. The feeling of a full stomach was thoroughly enjoyed. Then he would throw himself on the fresh dirt of the tunnel entrance and enjoy a series of very short, vigilant naps. Whistle-pigs have a great propensity for sleep. All members of this clan enjoy the pleasant feeling of the warm rays of the orb on their faces and on their backs. It is their way. They enjoy the physical sensation it gives to them. Adam definitely took delight in this feeling (especially with a full stomach), but he enjoyed it much more than that. It was a gift! A gift not to be just enjoyed but to be relished. It was both a physical sensation and a mental experience. He considered it an extension of the gift of his birth.

As he lolled in the warming rays, many thoughts flittered through his mind. Thinking was also very pleasant and rewarding to him, but it was also frustrating because he could not share! He often wondered about the departure. What was it? Where did those who experienced it go? He could not even ask the others. They could not understand, and there was no way for him to express it to them anyway. It is very frustrating indeed to be a prisoner in your own mind.

Sometimes the scent of the Sharp Nose Tribe would invade his nostrils. He would instinctively give the warning signal. As the others scurried to safety, Adam would scan for them and try to learn their ways. He knew that no sharp nose would dare to attack him. He was far too formidable and far too much of a risk for a member of that tribe to encounter. They knew the damage that he would inflict. Adam had a great resentment for them and would slowly and arrogantly lumber into his underground world.

Often as he foraged for food or explored or just lay there in his own, personal world, the winged clans would sing their songs. Now, there are two winged clans that all whistle-pigs highly value. The Large Noisy Clan and one of the crested clans were noisy clans indeed! They would give their non-melodic, singular-note "songs," which Adam considered noise, but when the notes came closer together, they were great oracles of danger. If any threat existed, they would erupt in their noisy chatter and begin to fly away. They were a valuable tool in the art of survival and therefore a valuable resource. They could see the sharp nose, and more importantly the two leg, when they were still far away. Eyes can see much better from the branch of an oak tree than from inches above the ground. They were indeed an ally!

Adam liked to listen to the small-winged clans, which his group had no interest in and so simply ignored. Their voices were truly songs. Most of the crested clans and the up-tail clans sang songs of goodness and the happiness

Ron L. Kuntz

of life. Their songs were especially useful when they were absent. They did not draw attention to themselves when danger lurked. Adam had already learned that. He loved to listen to them though.

Now, everyone knows that whistle-pigs cannot sing. There is no tempo in a whistle-pig's mind. In his mind, Adam sang their songs over and over! He wondered what they meant. Were they talking to each other? Sometimes he would be so enraptured that he would forget who he was and would try to grunt with them (There is very little tone and range in a grunt!). His head would bob as the notes coursed through his mind. This caused great concern amongst the other group members. Was Adam giving a warning? The tail moved in a strange fashion! Was there danger? They were confused as to what to do. Sadly, Adam had to cease this activity, but he still sang in his mind and continued to sing to his soul. Erato, the muse of poetry and song, would be pleased!

An activity none of his group was aware of was his nocturnal excursions. Sometimes when his restless mind would awaken him in the middle of the dark, he would venture forth from his burrow. The dark was a source of greatly increased danger. It was a time for the use of extreme caution and vigilance. Because of the increased peril, this behavior was a strong taboo. It was a time for the foolish! Whistle-pigs are not creatures of the dark. They are sleepers of the dark. Scents and sounds are enhanced because of the temperature and humidity, but vision for his kind is limited. The dark is a time for predators. Those who walk in the darkness need to take care! Adam did not fear. This was a whole new world to understand. Wonderment and discovery blunted any sense of danger.

He would lay and listen as the Ringtail Clan hunted in the small brook. They were seldom seen during the light. The Ringtail Clan was a clan of fierce hunters who feared none except the two leg. The ringtails were of no threat whatsoever to him. Tonight they hunted the Jumping Tribe and the pinchies. The Jumping Tribe seemed to be good only for startling Adam when he went down to the brook for a drink.

One light, Adam was at the edge of the little brook and idly flipped over a flat stone, as he once had seen a ringtail do. Lo and behold, there in the shallow water stood a pinchie! It was indeed a strange and alien-looking creature with the large, front legs each having two huge toes, and they both extended well beyond its head. The two antennae on the head also posed a mystery. Adam concluded that they must be very strange ears!

Of course, that always busy, button nose had to discover what scent a pinchie carried. The two toes on one of its front legs grasped on to that curious little twitcher! Adam raised his head and found that his crossed eyes had much trouble focusing on a creature that was so close. Then a sudden thought occurred to him—*it hurt!* On the second violent headshake, the pinchie released its grip and went flying to the safety of the middle of the tiny stream. It is said that as it flew back to the stream, it was smirking, but of course that most certainly could not be! The remainder of that light was spent in self-pity with many gentle, reassuring touches to his throbbing, offended friend. Adam's education was continuing, as he now had learned exactly why they were called pinchies!

During the dark, Adam's favorite activity (besides sleeping!) was to sit and gaze at the bright pinpoints of light that filled the blackness of the sky. What were they? Where did they go during the light? Did they have a burrow that they retreated to when the great, shiny orb arose from its slumber? So many questions! These puzzlements did not hinder the enjoyment of what he saw. It made it more so!

One dark, when the pinpoints were especially bright, Adam thought that it would be nice to take a few of the brightest and put them on the ceiling of his sleep chamber. So he went to the highest place on the hillside, stood as high as he could on his back toes, and stretched and reached and pawed. He felt foolish when he realized that they were even higher than the tallest of the oaks. Maybe it was best to let them stay so that all could enjoy them. He felt sorrow for those of his kind who never saw them!

One dark, as he sniffed his way back to the burrow, a repugnant odor assailed his nostrils. It was the scent of the Hairless Tail Clan. When he reached his den, it reeked of the stench of the hairless tail. As he began to enter, he came nose to nose with the hairless tailed one. The hairless exposed rows of needle sharp, white teeth and then gave a loud, formidable hiss that any of the Belly Crawler Clans would envy. The outpouring of breath considerably raised the stench level.

The Hairless Tail Clan do not dig their own lairs. They are instead takers by intimidation. Oh, they do have fearsome needle sharp teeth, but they are bluffers. Others of the Whistle-pig Clan would have retreated to another burrow, for they have many burrows. They are prolific diggers, and the more burrows, the shorter the avenue to escape and safety.

Adam knew the hairless tails were bluffers, and he was not in a giving mood. He bared his formidable, chisel-like front teeth and gave his best growl. His was not just a show of intimidation. This was not a bluff! The out-matched master of the bluff realized this in a heartbeat and fell over in a reasonable facsimile of a great departure. Adam knew that a departure had not taken place but was obligated to sniff and examine the seemingly lifeless body. Strangely, there was disappointment that the hairless had not departed and happiness that he had not been harmed. Grabbing the creature by the scruff of the neck, he tugged and pulled him to the tunnel entrance. At the top of the mound he used his head to give the limp enemy a roll down the hill. The hairless tailed one revived on the second roll, gave a final hiss, and scampered off.

Fortunately, the hairless had not entered deeply but had only marked the entrance as his own. The next hour was spent scraping out the contaminated dirt and shoving it over the hill—far over the hill! This clan was indeed a disgusting lot. Maybe this is why Adam's kinsmen gave up their dens so easily!

So it was that Adam's waking periods passed.

Life was passing.

Adam was happy, but often, Adam felt empty.

Vexation

IT WAS THE EARLY PART OF THE PLENTY PERIOD OF THE third cycle when tragedy would again befall Adam. One should learn from tragedy. In this regard, the members of the Whistle-pig Clan did well. If tragedy befell a clan member, the survivors, and especially the witnesses, became more wary and much more vigilant. Only the smallest-brained creatures do not learn from experience. Sometimes survival is bought at a high cost. Adam had a large advantage over the others. He learned fast, and he learned well!

Adam was also at a huge disadvantage. Tragedy may visit, but it should never be allowed to stay. If misfortune struck, the others may have learned from it, but the actual event was forgotten in several lights. Life went on—as it should! Adam dwelt on and relived those events over and over again. His two brothers had become very aware and very wary of the members of the Sharp Nose Tribe. They now did not know why or how they had acquired this advantage. They no longer remembered that their sister had ever existed. Adam remembered! Remembering is good only if the reason for remembering is good.

Whenever any of the three encountered their mother, a similar thing happened. All three brothers recognized the scent of their mother. It had been imprinted in their brains forever. For the two, she was a special member of the group. They did not truly know why she was special. They did not know that she was the one who had given them life. They no longer remembered she had provided them with warmth and food and protected them and taught them their basic skills. Vaguely they may have remembered that they lived together in the same burrow and that she had nipped their tail regions as she ousted them into the world. They really only knew that for some reason she was special. She also knew the scents of the three brothers. They were special to her, but that time had long passed. In a way though, they were still family.

Perhaps this is why the mother and the two brothers did not shun Adam as the others did. To the others, Adam was different, and he was to be avoided. When one is considered to be special, or if for any reason fondness exists or some unknown bond exists, faults are overlooked and even accepted. When any of the four would meet, a touching of noses and a tiny purr of recognition would always be in order. Is this not how it should be?

This light was one of the nicer for the beginning of the plenty period. It was cool, and the great orb was going in and out of the clouds. The orb was low in the sky yet but still felt wonderful on Adam's face. For the time period, it was a most excellent light. Adam wandered by the den his

Ron L. Kuntz

mother was using. He did not waddle as magnificently as he had done at the end of the cooling period, but he still waddled with the best.

His mother still used the burrow that Adam had been born in. He still considered this to be a special place and longed to enter and see it again, but he dared not. Mother had given birth to a brood only five lights ago. She may have considered him special, but an intrusion of her space at this time would not be tolerated. She would do much more than touch his little nose, and the purr would come with the chatter of her long, yellow-brown teeth. The reception would be ugly—quite ugly!

His ears were perked and attentive, and they heard faint, tiny sounds. He knew what those sounds were. He had made those same sounds three plenties ago. The tiny, wiggling nose detected the faint aroma of milk. His mind filled with memories. They were now vague and fuzzy memories, but they were warm memories. They were good memories! Again, it is impossible for any of the clan, or for any of the tribe, to smile. There are no muscles there to do it. Besides, can you imagine this flat, furry face beaming with four large, yellow buckteeth sticking out? I imagine the poster child for the dental association! So even if it were not visible, Adam was smiling as the pleasantness flooded his mind. There were new brothers and sisters in there! It was of no matter that they were probably half brothers and sisters. A deep longing came over him. There was a desperate need to see them, but it was mostly a desire to inhale their individual essences and commit them to his being.

But alas, this could not be done for at least twenty more lights. They were far too young and far too dependent to leave the birthing den. The grasses and leaves were far away in their future. Oh, and I should add that they would never be able to chuck wood!

The stirrings of Mother could be heard. She was starting to leave and go forage. It would not be good to be found even here. Adam scurried far from the entrance. The Whistle-pig Clan can actually scurry rather rapidly if there is a need. The waddle from their short legs comes so fast that an illusion of graceful speed is given. The wide body hides the short legs, and they look very much like a hovercraft. She would know that he had been there, and that would be bad enough. A world of woe awaited if he stayed!

From a distance and from cover, he watched her emerge. She was hungry and needed to replenish her milk supply, but caution had not been abandoned. It was some time before her emergence. Satisfying herself that no danger lurked nearby, she hurried to find the meager food supply. The period of plenty had barely begun, so she had to do with whatever she could find, and even this was far away. She had been going to the other side of the hill. This was not desirable but had become very necessary.

From his concealment, and being sure to remain motionless, Adam watched. He held no true love for his mother. They were on two different planes. But he was grateful for all that she had done and provided for him. The desire to watch her was stronger than the desire to fill his belly.

As she crested the hill, something strange happened. Suddenly, his mother jumped straight into the air. Then

Ron L. Kuntz

was heard a loud, sharp crack. It was much sharper and quicker and did not rumble like the noise that sometimes came from the sky, and the shiny orb was still beaming its rays. Something inside Adam told him to run, but he didn't. Something else in him said that his mother was in trouble and to go help, but he didn't. Even when he faintly heard the last breath in her lungs being expelled in a raspy, bubbly way, he didn't. There was danger there to be sure. Why? And how?

Before these questions could be answered, movement was seen in the distance. The animal that moved almost seemed to have no shape. It was a member of the Two Legged Tribe. It seemed to be wearing the meadow and forest itself! The two leg also carried a long, shiny stick with which he took great care. The orb made it flash in its rays.

As the figure approached his motionless mother, Adam wanted to signal danger with his stout little tail and to send an alarm so Mother could run and escape, but he didn't. Somehow he knew his mother had experienced the departure and was no longer there. The two leg stood over the mother and gave her a kick with his boot. As she rolled over, strange sounds came from the mouth of the two leg. He then turned and walked back to where he had been lying in wait. Adam memorized where the last motion was seen. When motion stopped, the two leg could no longer be seen, but he was surely there!

Very, very slowly, Adam backed deeper into the brush, all the time watching for movement. He did not understand how, but the two leg had been responsible for the great departure of his mother. They were to be carefully avoided, even at great distances. Even when wearing the skin of grasses and leaves, their motion and light flashes would betray them. When he had backed over to the other side of the hill, Adam hurried with all haste, trying to alert the group as he did. They were nowhere to be seen. They had all gone underground at the first sound of the sharp, loud noise.

The rest of the day was spent underground in safety. He knew that the loud noise was somehow responsible for the great departure. That he knew. What puzzled on his brain was why? She had not been taken back to the lair of the two leg as food for his pups like the sharp nose did. She had been left! Why? For whatever the reason was, he now was deprived of his mother.

As he finally fell asleep, Adam was very angry!

Ron L. Kuntz

The Guardian

BEFORE THE GREAT ORB PEEKED OVER THE HORIZON, Adam's eyelids fluttered. He awoke even though the den was in absolute darkness. Many animals have an inner alarm clock that regulates their lives. Adam was aware of the position of the orb even in his dark isolation. The memories of the last light flooded back to him. It was not a dream. It had truly happened!

The tiny paws were quickly placed beneath him, and he scrambled to the entrance. In his haste and lack of mental focus, caution was almost forgotten. He quickly regained his focus as the fresh air rushed into his nostrils. In a single moment, a lack of caution could equate to eternity.

The normal ritual of sniffing and listening and the slow emergence to the visual was again methodically observed. Actually, the emergence of today was much more closely adhered to. The great orb traveled far before he stood on the dirt mound.

When quite satisfied that this side of the hill was safe, he hurriedly found what he could eat before any other noses were poked above ground. Adam knew that the other side of the hill was a much better source of food. This was because it was much more open and the rays of the shiny orb fell there in far greater abundance. The Whistle-pig Clan has a strong tendency to construct their homes where the shrubs and trees offer cover and shadows in which to hide. In the shadows, the stout, grayish-brown bodies do not easily show a definite contour or shape. Standing out is usually not a great advantage in the animal kingdom! The openness of the bright side was in the favor of the two legs. The two legs could hurt and be dangerous from long distances.

When the other few of the group (The Whistle-pig Clan does not gather in large colonies as do the Prairie Clan.) began the short climb to the crest of the hill, they were met by a very animated and determined Adam. He knew that he could not convey his thoughts and ideas, but warn them he did! With stiff legs and tail, he paced in front of any who entertained the thought of gourmet dining. A sharp growl deep in the throat and a twitching tail were proving to be very effective.

Adam was shunned and perhaps disliked by his group. This was because they did not understand his differences. He might not be a normal clan member, but he was respected and feared by most. This morning, the eldest male was hungry and did not relish the idea of a second-rate breakfast. Ignorance can be a hindrance to intelligence! A challenge was in the making.

The legs and tail of the old male stiffened as he walked directly up to the barrier to a full and happy stomach. Whistle-pigs say much with their tails, and Adam read the message most clearly. Alas, for the old male, he was a creature of habit, and future actions were posted for all who could read. It is almost always a bluff, for this is not a clan renowned for its violence (everyone knew it!), and when the old male closed the distance to a foot or so, Adam acted with no warning. A sharp nip below the ear caused a little pain, but the surprise was overwhelming. This was not to be done in the ritual of confrontation! It was not fair! Adam had cheated! Turning and running, the old male decided that the sparse vegetation on the shady side of the hill was probably quite good and highly underrated. Schooling is the removal of hindrance to intelligence.

The sensation of victory was strong—and very sweet! Adam began to swagger (If one can waddle, one can swagger with the best!) to his burrow. But wait! Was there any real danger? It had to be confirmed, so he slowly made his way up to the ridge. If he was slow enough, there would be no visual stimulation of movement. He was stalking.

He arrived at the previous observation site. It was safe last night, but was it safe today? He looked for the exact spot the two leg had used and waited—and waited. Then in one spot, the leaves and grass moved. They moved to the site he watched and then ceased their movement. It must be the two leg! How wonderful it must be for a predator to have fur or skin like the plants! What an advantage! As he watched, a brief glint of light would occasionally wink from the spot. Was this the shiny stick the two leg carried?

Adam was motionless until the orb was high, as he watched and learned; then there was a sharp glint of light and the grasses moved. He could now determine the shape of the two leg. The grasses themselves seemed to stretch, and the two leg moved away in a steady, straight line. Even after the figure had gone over the next knoll, Adam still waited. This was a foe to be respected as well as to be feared. Then there was a cautious creeping forward to the hill's bright side and to the most prized plants as he carefully avoided the spot of his mother's departure. Adam gorged and filled his semi-empty belly. The plenty time was beginning to live up to its name, and the enemy was becoming known. He also had secured the reputation of the alpha male.

Adam was stuffed.

Adam was proud!

Ron L. Kuntz

Frustration

THE WADDLE HOME BECAME A VICTORY PARADE. THE belly was sated. The ego was sated. He was now the dominant male! He thought the walk. He waddled the walk! A proud little piggy was he—actually, he wasn't all that little! As he continued on his smug way, it became apparent that he was not headed home at all. He was making a rather wide detour in the direction of Mother's den. There was some puzzlement at that! He had not meant to do this and actually would have preferred to avoid this place as he had avoided the place of his mother's departure. He must have been very wrapped up in himself to do that. Still, he continued on and soon stood on the entrance mound.

Adam became uncomfortable there, and as he turned to leave, his ears detected the smallest of stirrings and voices. The brood! Of course! He must go see them and imprint their scents. As he slowly and cautiously made his way down to the birth chamber, there was a strong feeling of uneasiness. The swagger of moments ago had dissipated like the fog at mid-light. This was the tunnel that he had so anxiously tried to scamper out of almost three cycles ago. He knew that his original birth chamber would not be the same. With their penchant for digging, there is always constant alteration and renovation. Chambers are filled, and new ones are dug. Some passageways are enlarged, and others are closed. New entrances are dug, and old ones are abandoned. There are always multiple entrances to a den. It was strange that this one was still the same!

A feeling of awe overcame all other emotions as he timidly entered the birthing chamber. In the darkness, the nose and ears and sensitive front paws became his eyes. It was not necessary to see. There they were! His ears counted them as they squirmed in the dry grasses. There were four. *A good number!* he thought. His nose told him there were three males and one female. *A fine ratio!* He inhaled deeply, imprinting their likenesses forever onto his very soul. They were now a part of him forever! They were definitely his brothers and sister. Perhaps only half so, but that did not matter.

Very carefully, so as not to step on his tiny, animated brethren, Adam turned to leave. The brood had become much more active with the arrival of an adult. They squirmed now with much more intensity and purpose. He turned the corner to make the upward journey, the one that had brought a new world into his life three cycles ago. The light was dim and distant, yet his eyes blinked when they saw it.

The brood! What of them? Their mother had experienced the departure. No! *His* mother had experienced the departure! She was not to return! Panic surged through the little whistle-pig's brain. He wheeled and hurried back to his helpless brethren. Knowing not what to do, he placed a cold, twitching nose on each of them. The short little snout pushed and prodded and rolled them back together into the shallow depression Mother had made in the dried grasses and leaves. The shiny, black eyes darted here and there in the darkness where his ears and nose told him they would be. What was there for him to do? Food! Yes! It was food they wanted, and it was food they were in dire need of!

He raced out without the usual cautions that he always so methodically used. It was they who were in danger! Going from one burrow to the next, he searched for what was so urgently needed—a nursing female. There was only one in the small group, and she was not in the least bit interested. She had her paws full with her own brood, and what was not hers was not hers!

Now, Adam was the dominant male of this hillside, and all males gave way and did what their superior decreed. A female with nursing young was a whole different story! She was a whole different book! She was a whole different library! Adam did a very stupid thing (Remember, he was a male!). He followed her down the tunnel to her brood den. Upon reaching her young, she wheeled one hundred eighty degrees to face this trespasser. Adam had never heard such savage sounds and did not know that teeth could chatter so fast. She did not bluff! Immediately a hurting (She did more than chatter her teeth!) and startled Adam began to back up. The female bit and pushed the entire way to the entrance. It is amazing how fast the rear feet can backpedal if there is the proper motivation! It is also amazing how long it seems to take. At the entrance, a humbled whistle-pig turned and ran, and a satisfied whistle-pig returned to feed her young.

Adam knew that his mother's brood must be fed. He hurried back to the brood chamber. The four were quiet except for an occasional stirring or whimper. With no thought of himself, he went to the bright side of the hill and clipped the choicest and topmost parts of the grasses. Hastening back, he laid these in the nest. He positioned the food in front of the tiny faces and gently pushed their noses into it. No mouth opened to devour these delicacies. If some did enter a mouth, a little tongue immediately spat it out. No good!

He thought and thought and then, again with no precautions, went back to the far hillside. He clipped more of the tenderest vegetation. This he brought back and chewed into a soft, thick paste. He then tried to spit this into the now crying and yawning little mouths. A little choking and this too was refused. He had tried!

So Adam lay down and kept watch. For two lights and two darks he kept watch. He did not leave to fill his own belly, and even when his inner self knew that it was a dark, he did not sleep. It was a hopeless vigil, but he could not leave.

At the onset of the third light, the female departed. Adam's memory was flooded with images of far away and long ago. On the evening of the third light, the other three joined their sister. When the last breath was heard to leave and all had become quiet, Adam arose and sniffed

Ron L. Kuntz

and nudged each with a solemn, still little nose. All had joined the great departure. For a reason he did not understand, he was at peace. His brothers and sister no longer suffered. He thought that perhaps they had been reunited with his mother and were now being fed. Now maybe they were all happy and warm. It was a most comforting and happy thought!

He made one final check to see if the departure was complete, one final sniff, one final hope that they were happy, and he turned to leave.

There was one more thing to be done. None of the clan should ever enter this place, and for sure, none of the Hairless Tail Clan must ever find them. So turning his back, he dug dirt and stone from the floor and walls and covered his tiny kin. Then he sealed up the birthing chamber and went outside to do likewise to the three entrances.

As he sealed the last entrance, he noticed a large stone and tried with all his might to shove it over the entrance that he remembered so well and so fondly. It would not budge, so each entrance was marked with his scent. None would violate this mark as long as he existed!

A very tired, hungry, and sleepy whistle-pig went back to his own den and slept.

Adam was exhausted.

Closure

THE EYES COULD NOT BE SEEN IN THE BLACKNESS OF THE underworld when they suddenly popped open. Adam had slept the sleep of the departed. For two lights and two darks he had slept. There had been little, if any, stirring and no dreaming. It had been total sleep and rest. It was the sleep many long for but few achieve. Immediately, Adam's brain became a whirlwind of activity. All events of the previous days were relived.

It is impossible to know exactly why he awoke. Perhaps it was the faint singing of the winged clans as they greeted the onset of the light. Perhaps it was his serious thirst. Perhaps it was a sense of duty and unfinished tasks. Probably though, it was that tiny alarm clock planted countless generations ago, which always told the position of the great orb. It was still working quite well deep in the earth.

Adam scrambled to the entrance with its soft glow of the breaking light. His senses had returned and with them, the routine of safety. As he waited, he dwelt on his foolish and dangerous behavior of the past days. It had rained much during his long sleep, as it often does during the plenty period. The air smelled new and fresh. It was the type of air that carried the scents of not only the now plentiful flowers and blossoms but the scents of enemies as well.

With the rain had come increasing warmth, and now the earth was rapidly awakening as if it had been reborn. The hurrying paws made a soft, cushy sound as they contacted the wet vegetation and a squishy one as they came down upon the bare spots. When he arrived at the birthing den, relief at what he saw drowned out all other thoughts. It was still sealed! In the muddy, bare ground, there were many paw prints. Members of the group had been there. A ringtail had skirted to the outside. They were always curious! At the entrance he saw many tracks of the Hairless Tail Clan. They were always hungry and always opportunistic, but they had not dug. The markings of a dominant male are respected by most of the tribes and clans.

With the rains, it would be wise to freshly mark this forbidden zone again. A poor effort indeed! He had forgotten that not only had he not eaten for several lights, but he had not drunk any water, either. With this realization, he was consumed by his need for water and food. He ran to the risen brook and drank and drank of its sweet water. It is said that the brook ran not as high or as fast when he had finished. When he had finally satisfied his considerable thirst, he stood to look for food. A combination of the sloshing of his belly, the feel of the soft mud oozing between the toes, and the plenty that had so rapidly grown caused a broad smile. One cannot actually see the Whistle-pig Clan smile, but this time I'm not too sure! It was the first one since the encounter with the two leg. It felt good!

Food was now everywhere! Even the shady side of the hill had exploded into a land of plenty with the tender shoots of new growth. The plenty period was now living up to its name. It should also be noted that there was not nearly as much of this tender new growth when Adam had finished. He smugly looked at the result of his gluttony, and the grin returned. This time the grin was bigger and even more satisfied!

Now, to find a drier spot and bathe in the warm gift of the great orb. Full, warm, and content, he began to doze. Now how, you may ask, can anybody or anything sleep after such a long and deep and almost coma-like sleep? Well, this clan has a great talent not only for digging but for sleeping as well. They are amongst the best in these two areas! So he dozed. It was a light and vigilant sleep. The sleep periods were only moments long. In and out of the embrace of Morpheus he went. Between these he thought of the goodness of the water, the taste of the food, and how good it was that the den had not been disturbed.

As the images of the sealed entrance fluttered through his content little mind, a horrible thought overwhelmed him. The tracks in the mud! His mother!

There was a pronounced increase in the waddle as he hurried to the top of the hill. First, however, came a stop at the birthing den. He could now re-mark this territory.

He did this in profusion and perhaps with a little gusto! Now to the top of the hill.

Caution! Caution! Caution! When the crest was reached, movement became slow and deliberant. Shadows were skillfully taken advantage of. It was as if the two leg was being stalked! He could now see where the two leg had hidden in ambush. No movement or shiny reflections could be seen. Perhaps since no prey had been here for several lights, the two leg had left to look for a better hunting ground. As Adam crept to the place of his mother's departure, all senses keenly and warily scanned for the signs of the master predator. There were none.

Upon arriving at the exact spot, an amazing, although not unexpected, discovery was made. Mother was no longer there! With the many passing lights and the rain, barely a slight, lingering scent remained. Adam shuddered. He knew that all of the plants and animals were a source of food, and therefore life, to some other creature. It was the way! All things were to follow the way. As he pondered the next action to find her, an errant breeze told the little nose all. He had often caught this repulsive smell. In the past its source was avoided. Now he followed the breeze and its odor back to its origin. Some clans found this odor obnoxious, and to some clans it was an opportunity. To Adam, it was repulsive, but it had to be followed.

The trail ended forty yards up a seldom-used path. There he found a scattering of bones, some rotting skin and fur, and little more. There was not even enough for the maggots to feast upon. There was, however, enough scent to identify. Adam lay there in the repugnant air and paid homage as early memories of her care flitted through his mind. A grin appeared as he thought of her rolling him back down to the others. He had an obligation to her, and he paid it as best he could. The hairless tails probably would not return. During the plenty period, this was not enough for even them to bother with. Turning his back, he began to throw dirt and leaves over the remains. He was indeed grateful to her for his existence. This place Adam would never again visit.

As the dark began, Adam felt great sadness as he curled up in his nest of dried leaves. He did not know where his mother had departed to. He thought that he would never see her again but hoped with all his heart that she was okay and content somewhere. Suddenly, an image was impressed upon his troubled mind. It was of Mother in a land of abundant food and no enemies. She tended to her babies, and they were growing up and thriving. She was smiling!

Adam fell asleep.

Adam was at peace.

The Floppy

ADAM WAS LOOKED UPON AS ONE WHO HAD STRANGE ways in regard to the clan lifestyle. This might be overlooked, but it was his mental and physical powers that were the most troubling to the others. Respected? Definitely! Avoided? If at all possible! Ironically, it was Adam who felt the most uncomfortable when in the company of the group. There was a strong desire to fit in and belong, but he simply did not and could not fit in. He had become a hermit, and it was time to move on. This was no longer a place where happy memories could be made.

So he thought and searched and thought and searched some more. Specifications had to be met. His future home was to be an estate. It was to be a fortress. It was to be a castle. It was, unfortunately, also to be a hermitage! The perfect site was finally found. It was a short distance from the group but in a direction so that contact could easily be avoided if desired. There were shrubs and small trees to guard against any long-range danger. This was the danger that was now the most feared. The new site was also airy, where even the gentlest of breezes swirled in from all directions. This would vastly reduce the short-range stalking dangers. There were also two features that were truly desired, and yes, needed, to be happy. The bright orb shone on his mound at the very beginning of the light, and there was a most wonderful view of the trail. He was alone, but he was not lonely. Adam had his thoughts, and remember, all his life he had really always been alone. So it was that the palace was dug, and many lights were spent lining its chambers with a thick layer of the softest of the leaves and grasses. As a finishing touch, dried blossoms and flowers were added.

Part of each day was spent basking and thinking. Many of the small-winged clans would favor him with their songs. It was a time of pleasantry and comfort, and much of this time was spent thinking on the puzzlements of his existence.

Now, let it be known that members of the Whistle-pig Clan are a peace-loving clan! Their four favorite physical activities are: 1) eating, 2) sun basking, 3) sleeping, 4) digging, and 5) eating. (Let it also be known that there are three kinds of whistle-pigs: Those that count and those that can't count, and Adam was definitely all three kinds!) Fighting is far down the list. Heck! Fighting isn't even on that list! Bluffing, however, is somewhere toward the bottom. You must also be made aware that if any are forced into an argument that cannot be bluffed or avoided, they will hunker down and vigorously defend their position. Only the most hungry (or the most stupid) will enter into a one-on-one debate with a fully grown, healthy, male clan member, especially one as large as Adam! Besides, he did not always follow the accepted rules that were developed over countless generations. He knew the rules quite well. They were deeply embedded into his very being, but...well—he cheated! In his defense, it must be said that he often cheated fairly!

Adam actually loved to do the contrary! Any diversion from the ordinary was to be savored and enjoyed to the utmost and then relived over and over again. For instance, if a member of any of the Belly Crawler Clans was found near his estate, he took delight in kicking dirt at it until it hissed angrily and slithered away. There was definitely an ornery streak in the lad!

So it was that on a bright, shiny, orb-dominated light, nearing the middle of the cooling period, Adam became acquainted with a member of the Barking Tribe. This one was a member of the Floppy-Eared Clan, and he was actively engaged in trying to find a member of the Long-Eared Clan. The long ears belonged to a far removed clan of the chisel tooths. Sometimes Adam questioned if they were a relation at all. At least they minded their own business!

The floppies loved to hunt and chase the long ears. It seemed to be what they lived for. They dug, they ate, they slept, and they basked, but the hunt and the chase was always number one on their list. A curious thing about floppies was that they hunted only for the sport of it. They did not hunt for their survival. It was a good thing too, because they never caught anything! How could they? They always made such a noise as they chased, and the long ears were ever so much faster! They were curious indeed! Adam thought that they should definitely work on their stalking technique.

The ever-active nose of this floppy had been trolling the sides of the trail when it picked up something very interesting. This new scent trail had only to be followed a few feet, and there stood Adam! Minding his own business! Bothering no one! Doing his number one favorite activity! It became extremely obvious that it was indeed time to retreat to the fruit of his number four favorite activity. But alas, his fastest run (an imitation of a fat hovercraft) was no match for even the short legs of this highly motivated floppy.

In whistle-pig fighting, rule number one is to never be caught from behind. Adam abruptly halted his retreat and turned to face the cause of his meal interruption. Rule number one obeyed! Good Adam! Rule number two is to never let an enemy get behind you. This clan does not turn with the rapidity of many of the other clans. The solution is simple: back up to a bush or tree or rock so nothing can get behind you. The long, sharp chisel teeth are a far better defense than a stout little tail, no matter how fast it moves. The tail was now backed up to a hawthorn bush. Rule two obeyed! Good Adam!

Rule number three is to put on a good bluff. Most wild animals will not risk an injury. An injury in the wild is often a slow death sentence from infection or starvation. So the ears were flattened, the stout tail wagged furiously, and the long, yellow teeth were bared as they chattered loudly and most fiercely. This was accompanied with guttural growl-

Ron L. Kuntz

ing and a vicious snarl. It was an effective ploy! The floppy could not advance, and Adam could not retreat. It had become an interesting standoff. There was no violence, but it was a grand and loud show of growling, barking, and teeth snapping. Rule number three obeyed! Good Adam!

He found it fascinating that the floppy was playing by his rules. The floppy would bark, show its teeth in a growl, lunge forward, and snap its teeth. When this occurred, Adam would oblige by recoiling backward so the teeth snapped about six inches in front of his stiff little nose. Then Adam would chatter his teeth, growl, and also lunge forward, with the floppy jerking his head backward. Now, please understand that if Adam were old, or young, or sick, or already impaired by an injury, this would be fought under far different rules and would have a most different outcome! Adam, however, was beginning to enjoy this game. It was exciting, and he was in no real danger. Besides, his existence had become a solitary and uneventful one, and this was a grand relief from the daily routine!

Then his laid back ears heard it! It was the voices of the dreaded two legs. Their voices were excited and were rapidly moving toward the sounds of this noisy encounter. He was in serious trouble now! The huge teeth ceased their machine-gun-like chatter. In response, the lunges of the floppy came ever nearer to the precious little nose, which had now started some serious activity. The bark and then the growl heralded the advent of the lunge. As the next sequence began, Adam waited for the growl and the beginning of the mouth opening. Instead of a single lunge forward, there were two lunges forward. The advantage was firmly in favor of the one who knew where the other would be. The razor sharp incisors caught the floppy's cheek right before the snap. Adam had cheated! Bad Adam? Even as the teeth came together there came a yelp of pain and surprise. At this point, however, it was mostly surprise. Then came a frantic retreat. It would be more accurate to say it was an attempt at a retreat. Movement can definitely be hindered by something half of your weight attached firmly to your jowl! With a final shake of his head for good measure, Adam heard a louder and more urgent howl and released his grip.

As the bloodied animal ran in the direction of the now even more excited two legs, Adam scurried to his den. At the entrance he paused and turned to watch the trail. His heart pounded and his mind reeled. He felt proud! It was great to play with a new friend! With only his head slightly visible, he watched and listened as the floppy reached his masters. He knew floppies were the slaves of the Two Leg Tribe. They were happy with this arrangement and were quite dependent on them. It was their way.

There were loud shouts as they examined the damage that had been inflicted. Then he heard strange growling from the two masters of the floppy. They were surely not happy with what he had done. Adam watched as the two legs turned and began the trip back up the trail with the ego-damaged floppy meekly following behind them with head down. The masters continued their strange growling with each other until well out of sight.

It was the first time Adam had ever heard laughter!

Adam was hungry!

Ron L. Kuntz

The Sharp Nose

THE NEXT THREE CYCLES WERE SPENT VERY PLEASANTLY in Adam's country estate. They were pleasant from a physical point of view. They were also frustrating. There were troubling images of the past and so many puzzlements he could not solve. The biggest enigma of all was to not be able to share his thoughts and to remain a prisoner in his own mind. A sense of not belonging and unfulfillment smoldered still in his heart.

The rising orb of the late plenty period shone warmly on Adam's fur as he sprawled on the dirt mound of his burrow. The warmth on his face and back was a great contrast to the coolness he felt on his belly. The Whistle-pig Clan has very little hair on their underside. It was quite satisfying.

Adam had already eaten his fill and was trying not to doze. This was the beginning of his sixth cycle. He would rapidly pass his prime and soon begin his feeble time. For now, though, he still looked like a magnificent specimen of pig-hood. Still bigger than most, he was recovering from the inactivity and the fast of the sleep. He was beginning to gray, and his joints ached. Old age was very soon to be. Perhaps this would be his last good cycle. Perhaps two or three more, but on this he did not dwell.

For a reason unknown to him, his eyes were suddenly wide open and focused. There was movement only a short distance away. He saw a large, pointed ear turn and flutter. The alarm was immediately sounded. This sharp nose would not be successful in the group, at least not today. The young were all quickly hidden safely away!

Adam was now alone. There was a strong urge to join his clan-mates. *This is strange*, he thought. There was no fear of this lone sharp nose. The sharp nose only preyed on the old and the sick and the young. A healthy adult male was far too formidable a foe for a single sharp nose. It was still the plenty time, a time of abundance, and this sharp nose was surely not desperate. It was only opportunistic.

There was no fear, and he fought off his inner urge to run and hide. He knew that the sharp nose only did what it had to do. It could not eat the clover and bark and roots that were provided. It had to eat flesh. It was the way. Adam gave a shiver and gave thanks that he was what he was.

The sharp nose no longer moved and could now not be seen. It would easily be seen by most of the two legs. The rising orb would make the shiny red coat visible. As mentioned, the Whistle-pig Clan is color blind and can only see shades of gray. The greenery of the shrubs and grasses were of the same shade of gray as the red of the sharp nose.

Adam became uneasy as he looked for the motionless foe. Nervously deciding it was better to join the group, he

Ron L. Kuntz

turned to amble into the burrow. He would not scurry! With a slight change in the early breeze, the sharp nose scent entered the twitching nostrils. He stopped his turning. Adam had smelled the sharp nose many, many times before, but this time something was different. This particular scent brought back memories. The mists of time parted as this scent became crystal clear. It was familiar from long, long ago. But who? Or when? Or where?

It was slammed back into memory by his young sister's final squeals of pain and horror. Although it was over six cycles ago, it was permanently preserved in his mind. He became engulfed in an emotion he had never truly experienced before. It was hate and a thirst for revenge! He burned with it as he relived that morning so long ago over and over again. As a pup he had only experienced fear and panic. Now he experienced hate. It was a deep, overwhelming emotion! This was the one!

Adam turned to locate the object of his hatred. He saw nothing, but the breeze told him what he wanted to know. The location was no longer a secret. He would now charge this hated creature and sink his long, chisel-like front teeth deep into the neck of the red one. It did not matter what Adam's fate would be. His only thought was to hurt, or better yet, destroy, this creature. *But this cannot be done*, he sadly thought. Adam was quick, but the red one was the master of agility and quickness. If he moved forward to do battle, an animal as smart as the red would never engage such a large, healthy adult. There was surely no profit in that. In times of plenty, it would only stalk and attack a very young, very old, or very sick whistle-pig. Predators only like easy prey that will do them no damage.

A thought passed through Adam's mind. It was a wonderful thought! Play the game! As told before, whistle-pigs cannot smile. Adam smiled. It was a slightly crooked grin to be sure, but it was a smile. It was actually a crooked, wicked, evil smile.

He began to walk directly toward his enemy. The red one did not move. There was no present danger to her at all. The red and the gray attacked only from behind. In this manner they would avoid the teeth and have an easy opportunity to grab the nape and quickly crush the neck vertebrae.

Adam's front legs suddenly buckled, and he fell on his chin. The red one's ears pricked to their highest, and her eyes shone intently with anticipation. Visual clues are important stimuli to their instincts, not their intelligence. Adam's smile broadened. As his chin touched the grass, there was a sharp squeal of pain. The red one was now on her feet. Instincts are the powerful driving forces in the animal world.

There were many soft cries of pain on the journey back. This was in concert with much limping and falling. It was an excellent performance, and if the animal kingdom gave awards, there would be an Emmy or perhaps even an Oscar nomination in this offering.

Adam's instincts and senses were in full swing. He could feel that the stalking had begun, and he could hear the distance closing. With much difficulty, the urge and instinct to run was suppressed.

At seven body lengths, the red made her run and lunge, which had worked so well during her eight cycles. The strategy was known, and Adam swirled to meet her. The red one missed her mark and had to settle for Adam's right paw and foreleg. As her teeth found their way into and through the paw, Adam's teeth clenched on her foreleg joint. It would equate to the elbow of a two leg. The red one emitted a high shriek of both surprise and pain and immediately released her hold. Adam gripped all the harder and could feel and hear his teeth clench together. He also experienced a taste like none before. It was not like the floppy. The taste of this blood he reveled in. He gave a mighty shake and then let his totally surprised aggressor go. The red jumped into the air and collapsed to the ground when her foreleg would not support her. She ran, severely limping, into the brush.

Adam felt no pain. He felt only redemption and victory. He had done it! As he watched the red one limp out of sight with her foreleg dangling only to the vertical, he became aware of a terrible throbbing in his right paw. Instinctively, he licked the paw. The taste was not as sweet as the blood of the red one. He hurriedly limped into his burrow.

As he licked the paw, he noticed one of the toes was missing and the others were badly mangled. Even with the pain and the realization that his paw would never be of use again, he was jubilant. He went to his lair.

With the badly injured paw in front of his mouth and licking tongue, he curled up in a tight ball and relived his battle over and over again. Each time he was victorious! When sleep finally conquered his active mind, the body would shake and the tiny legs would twitch as they replayed the events of the day.

Adam was satisfied.

New Eyes

IN THE INKY BLACKNESS OF HIS LAIR, ADAM'S EYES POPPED open before the orb had appeared on the horizon. That instinctive, preset alarm again functioned perfectly. As he awoke, he uncoiled and put his little paws beneath his fat body in order to stand. A searing jolt of pain coursed up from the mangled right foreleg to behind his beady, black eyes! The eyes snapped tightly shut, and his entire body recoiled in pain and surprise at this unexpected sensation. Adam was startled! Then his memory became flooded with the images of the last light. The pain was now not as intense—at least it became easier to tolerate.

After limping the upward journey into the light, the morning ritual of munching began. There were numerous interruptions to this most sacred of rites. There was much more time spent licking and cleaning and assessing the damaged limb than in the munch. The paw hurt badly and had been damaged far beyond repair. With constant licking and cleaning it would heal. Adam knew there

Ron L. Kuntz

would always probably be pain, or at best a nagging, constant soreness. This could be tolerated. The pain would remind him of his victory, and when he left paw prints, all would know that it was he who had been there!

He could still survive. The leg was useless for digging. That was no problem. He already had his castle dug and well furnished. A few alterations could be handled. A wry, cynical smile formed at the thought that digging the guest sleep chamber could be postponed. He would never run well again. No problem there! He never could run well, and there would always be a safe haven nearby. Food would also be no problem. A piece of bark or a tasty clover blossom did not run very fast, and he could still stand and reach just as high as ever. Yes, he would survive and do fine.

The cynical smile returned to his mind. What of the red one? The smile broadened as he remembered her cry of pain as his teeth sliced through the joint. His mind could hardly contain the enormity of the grin when picturing the vanquished one trying to run away with the useless foreleg dangling wildly in all directions.

The smile began to fade as he wondered about her fate and what he had truly done. A new emotion was forming in the little piggy brain. It was an emotion he tried very hard to suppress but could not. It was pity! How can pity be given to one who had none? The red one was surely doomed. She would slowly but very surely join in the departure. She not only depended upon stealth but upon quickness and speed. Now she had none of these. Adam's prey did not move, except to sway in a breeze. The smile returned as he pictured how funny it would be to watch her trying to run down a long ear, even an old or sick one! The red one was doomed!

Try as he might, the pity returned. It was now forming an alliance with sorrow. That was not fair! An injury caused by their prey, no matter how small, could mean very hard times for a predator, hard times not just for themselves but for their families as well.

Did the red female have pups in her den? This was the right period. Would they experience a horrible departure also? This thought brought a shiver to Adam as events from his past were relived. Her pups had done no wrong. She hadn't either. She had only done what was required of her. The pointy noses were not cowards. They did not prey upon the old and sick and young out of cowardliness. They did so because they had to. The red one did what nature had commanded her to do. She never had committed an evil as Adam had always imagined. She had only followed the way.

Now regret joined the alliance of pity and sorrow in their persistent attack. Had Adam done an evil thing? It had not been necessary to do what he had done. It was not the way! Now his mind pictured her coming back to the den, light after light, with nothing to give her hungry offspring. Would she watch their departure, or would they one day have her not return to them? No matter how hard Adam tried to shake these thoughts and images from his mind, they would always return.

The other group members were now beginning to emerge from their tunnels of safety. The adults poked twitching noses out first. Upon seeing Adam, their emergence was greatly accelerated. If one of their group was above ground, then it must be safe. One by one, the bravest first (or the youngest) were drawn to the smells of yesterday's battle. Nervously, their tiny, twitching noses beheld the stale odor of the dried blood of both combatants. They quickly backed away. They then did the same to the badly mangled paw, and the results were the same.

As they waddled away, Adam longed to tell them of his valor and details of his victory but was frustrated at the total failure to communicate. They only knew that something they did not want to know about had happened and that Adam was hurt. They soon lost interest in both.

Anger now took on the alliance of three. How ungrateful! He was a hero! He had rescued them! He had delivered them! He was their savior! Where was their gratitude? They only cared that they were safe and they now could fill their bellies and sun themselves. Adam was disgusted with his clan.

In the long term, anger can be (and should be!) a fleeting and poor opponent to regret, compassion, and sorrow. That dark, as he tucked the throbbing paw beneath him, he felt very foolish for the thoughts he'd had that morning. It was another of the few times he was glad that none could understand him. He felt sorrow for his thoughts and felt sorrow for the Red Clan family. They had done no wrong. They were without blame. The red one had done nothing that she did not have to do. She had followed the way. Perhaps maybe an enemy is just someone you don't understand.

Anger then tried for a comeback. He felt anger toward all the Sharp Nose Tribe. He was angry with his group. He was especially angry with himself.

That dark, as sleep tried to come, Adam was confused!

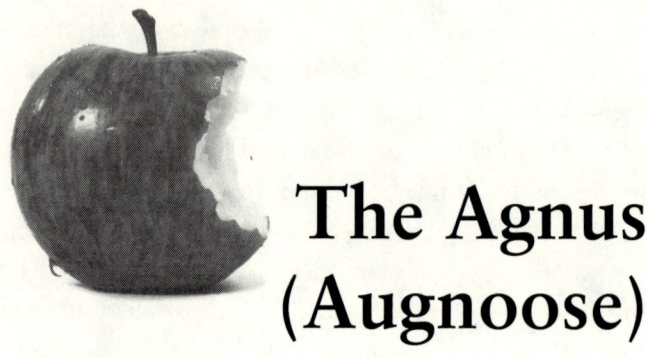

The Agnus (Augnoose)

Adam lay sprawled on the bare dirt in front of his burrow. It was very, very late in the cooling period, and the shiny orb had little warmth to give. The sleep period was close at hand, so even this meager warmth was welcome. Adam had lived through six of these. Perhaps it may be better to say that he had survived six of them! Not many of his kind survive seven. His bones and especially his paw hurt, and he knew it would be much worse when he awoke. He was weary—very weary. There was no choice but to endure this departure-mimicking sleep.

He was not as ready as he had been in past cycles. His fur was not as sleek and thick, and he did not waddle as in previous cooling periods. There was concern that not enough fat had been stored to insulate him from the cold and to supply his energy. During the late cooling period

Ron L. Kuntz

there was little food, at least of the type Adam favored, but that did not matter. Even if the land was as it is during the plenty period, there would still be little desire to eat. Adam did not feel hunger; he felt acceptance.

Idly, he watched a large member of the Belly Crawler Tribe who lay coiled on a large, flat rock. It also was enjoying those last precious moments of warmth. This particular one belonged to a clan that was not to be messed with, at least not by any normal whistle-pig. They were not as dangerous as the Noisy Tail Clan, but they were to be avoided by any sane beast. This was one that Adam had played with long ago. Adam mulled over the idea of going over and again playing with him. Belly crawlers all had such an attitude problem! They never wanted to play! Adam had a strong dislike for anything with an attitude. It might be fun to go over there and kick some dirt in its face!

This light, the crawler was saved. It was just too pleasant to get up and move right now, and Adam noticed it had recently suffered a rather serious wound. Its tail was severely damaged, and the end was actually missing. Adam was ornery but not mean. Adam wondered if it had been the winner and what clan would be so desperate to do this to one so dangerous.

From afar, a white speck was moving slowly on the trail toward him. Adam was too comfortable to move and somehow felt there was no need to do so. These last moments of warmth were too comforting to his bones to give up so easily. As the figure came closer, it was seen that the two leg carried a stick. It was not a shiny stick and was not being carried as he had seen the other two legs do. It was only being used to navigate the rocky trail.

A strange serenity came over him. There was still no urge to turn and scurry into the safety of his fortress. Was it the warmth of the orb? Did he not want to begin the sleep period? Was he simply too old to care? The answer came to him! He felt no danger from this two leg, and besides, even in his present condition, escape would be quick. So he lay motionless as the figure came within a short distance. The stranger had to see him, even though there had not been even a twitch of the usually active little nose.

The stranger looked down upon the belly crawler, and the belly crawler gave a nasty hiss and looked directly into the eyes of the two leg. For a few moments, both were locked in a stare-down over possession of the rock. The crawler was the first to blink (I am aware that it had no eyelids, but it did happen! Remember, I also told you whistle-pigs can't smile.). It slithered off into the bushes.

The stranger sat down upon the disputed flat rock, using the wooden stick for support. Their eyes became locked into a soul-searching stare. A strange thing then happened. The two leg smiled (Some two legs are able to actually physically smile!), touched his beard, and said, "You have been a fine whistle-pig, and I am very pleased with you." It came as a total surprise! How was it that Adam knew what was said? He knew no language of the two leg! How did he hear? There were no sounds that his ears heard! The claws on the back legs dug into the hard clay, ready to turn him into the safety of the burrow. The ears were now laid back on the side of the head. Again, without a sound being made, Adam was told not to be afraid. And he wasn't! He again felt no danger and was very much at peace.

How was it that this stranger could talk to him without speaking? "You have many questions, little one, and many shall be answered today." Adam had made no noise! Not a purr, not a chortle, not even an audible breathing sound! This two leg had known what was in his heart and mind! Then it occurred to Adam that he was having a conversation and exchanging thoughts and ideas. It was wonderful! It had never happened before and had always been his greatest wish. He was no longer a prisoner! How it was happening did not matter!

For lack of a better term, I shall say they talked.

A new friend, especially such a wonderful one, must be called something. Besides, his friend had no scent, and the term two leg was a term Adam used in contempt. The brow of the stranger furrowed and told him that although he was called by many names, a good one for Adam to use would be Agnus. Adam thought it was a strange thing for a name, but then Adam had never used a name before. Maybe it was what the two legs called each other. But if his friend wanted to be called that, then it was a most excellent name! Agnus smiled at that. He was pleased.

Then they talked! They talked of the small-winged clans and the pleasure they brought with their songs. They talked of the warmth of the shiny orb and the beautiful dots of light during the dark. Adam did not understand what they were, but more wonderments were given for him to puzzle over. Many things were talked of, many that, unfortunately, are taken for granted or seem trivial to others. Then his mother and sister were asked about. What had happened to them? To this, Agnus replied that Adam had already been told.

As a fleeting thought of shame flashed through his churning little mind, the right hand of Agnus raised immediately. "Do not feel guilt any longer for what happened to the Red Clan female. She belonged to me, and her departure was surely not in vain." With that, Agnus made an actual sound, which puzzled Adam. Suddenly, there was movement from beside the trail. From seemingly nowhere sprang two young Red Clan members, and they charged directly for them! How stupid he had been! Adam had been so rapt that he had not noticed that they had been stalked. He immediately wheeled to disappear into his burrow for safety.

But what of his new friend? There was no sheltering burrow to offer Agnus safety! Only the Antlered Clans could outrun the red ones. Adam wheeled back to his original position and moved to block the path of the attackers. Adam was not, at his age and condition, a match for one determined red one. He knew this well, and also that there would be no doubt as to the outcome with two members of this nimble clan. But this was acceptable! He would give Agnus time to flee to safety, or at worst, satisfy the need for flesh that the red ones desired. This was not to be a bluff!

Agnus turned to him and held up a hand. Adam was no longer able to move and watched helplessly in horror as the distance rapidly closed. *Run! Run! Please run! Use the stick!* His friend was bowled over from the sitting position as the two completed their charge. His face and neck had been targeted as expected. Strangely, there were no cries of pain and no snarls—at least, no meaningful ones. Adam's pricked ears heard what he now knew as laughter and sounds like he made as a pup when tumbling with his sister and brothers when Mother was foraging. The red ones licked the face of Agnus. Were they tasting? No! The licks resulted in more and stronger laughter. They were playing! Another sound from Agnus and the two sat and watched with bright puppy eyes.

Now Agnus looked intently at Adam. The brood of the red female had survived and flourished. There was happiness and joy to be found here, not sorrow. She had been happy to see her ambition come to a conclusion. Her destiny had been fulfilled, and her legacy still lived. There was no anger or ill feelings. It was not the way. Then Agnus looked the two young reds in their eyes and gave a slight nod. The two turned toward Adam and slowly approached him. He still was unable to move but felt no need. There was no fear as they nuzzled his face and nape, purring and whining as they did so.

Agnus then gave a sharp, command-like noise, and the two came to a full state of alert. They were now agitated and seemed very nervous. Their manner had gone from loving and playful to one of nervous apprehension. Agnus pointed up the valley, and both bounded away. There was not even a single glance back as they raced away. A feeling of peace descended upon Adam as he watched the twin bushy tails disappear into the brambles.

When he turned back toward his new friend, Agnus began to speak of a female whistle-pig who lived in the next valley. Adam's mind was still on the two Red Clan members. The mind came to full attention when it was said that she was very much like him. Was there another like him? She also was frustrated at not being able to communicate with her group. It was her dream as well. She had never taken a mate and therefore had never raised a litter. She had also been shunned by her group because of her behavior and had been forced to live apart. Yes, she was a most unhappy little whistle-pig. Adam identified! She was like him! Adam's nose twitched faster and faster, and his tail stiffened and began to sway.

But alas, she was now old and sickly and had given up on her existence. What else was there to know? Adam needed to know everything! There was a pause at that request, and with a gleam in both eyes, Agnus said, "Only that she has a very nice scent." Adam's tail now wagged furiously! He caught the gleam in his new friend's eyes and immediately seized the movement. Now, it is a fact that whistle-pigs do not blush. It is indeed an impossibility! But Adam was indeed blushing as his embarrassment increased. At least he had not whistled!

Agnus laughed a most wonderful laugh. It was melodious like the small-winged clans sing in the plenty period. It was loving and spoke of life. It was full of love. There was no derision or fun making as was done to the floppy. Adam found himself making clucking noises in response.

Would the female survive the sleep period? Often the old and the sickly face the great departure during this trying time. He must see her! He must communicate with her! Agnus solemnly promised to return when Adam's great sleep was done and that he would be taken to visit the female of the nice scent. Adam was delighted and vigorously shook his tail rapidly from side to side. There was no longer any embarrassment. When his sleep period was over, would his future friend still be there, and would his new friend really return? A cloud of doubt was building in his mind. Agnus again made the promise, and Adam believed!

What of the legacy of Adam? Mother's legacy had been fulfilled. There were many descendants of hers in the nearby hills. There were three sons, many grandchildren, and too many in other generations to count. She had gone on the great departure, but she was still here. But what of Adam? A sadness began to overtake him as he heard that his legacy had done nicely. A serious look came upon the face of Agnus, and some strange things were then said. He was pleased with Adam for all the cycles of his existence. How? The time of knowing was short! The shiny orb had not yet completed its journey back to its burrow. They met much less than half a light ago. Then Agnus said something even stranger. He said that Adam had cared for him when he was sick and in need. Adam decided that this could not be true, but there was now comfort deep in his heart.

It had become time to part. Agnus stood up and looked down the little valley and then down upon his lifelong friend. He knelt to one knee and put two fingers to his mouth. He then placed the fingers on Adam's right paw, saying that he knew the pain a severe injury to a paw could cause. Adam knew that this also could not be so. No tribe would harm one as good as this. The two legs would not harm one of their own! He had seen the sharp noses love him. Even the hairless tails, who ate the decayed remains of those who had experienced the departure, would surely respect Agnus! "Do not judge!" was the reply to these thoughts.

As he started to regain his feet, there was a hesitation, then a smile, and a finger was placed on Adam's nose. The tiny nose began a frantic, almost frenzied twitching. It was desperate to capture the scent of this two leg for his memory.

This pleased Agnus very much! He laughed a laugh that was of pure delight, and his eyes twinkled. "You are truly not only a wise whistle-pig but a good and delightful one besides. I am pleased, and I shall visit you soon again."

As he turned to leave, he hesitated and turned back to face his little friend. A wonderful, loving (perhaps mischievous) smile came to his face, and he said, "When I told the female of you and that she would meet you after her sleep was finished, her tail thumped faster than yours!"

Adam was beyond delight!

Ron L. Kuntz

Omega

ADAM WATCHED AS HIS NEW FRIEND WALKED SLOWLY down the path. Two figures were coming up the path toward him. They were two legs, and it could now be seen that they both carried the shiny sticks. They were hunting. It was obvious to Adam that it was not he whom they hunted. They were not wearing the skins of grasses and leaves, and they were making far too much noise. Their words and laughter were bright and loud. They also had with them a floppy, who ran ahead using his broad nose on everything. Adam wondered if this was his floppy and smiled as he relived their encounter, but the wind blew down the path so he could not be sure. They were probably hunting the long ears today. That's what floppies loved best! As the distance closed, he had a fleeting worry for his friend. He then remembered that the Two Leg Tribe would surely never harm one of their own and felt better as he watched. Somehow he knew that the stick Agnus carried was more powerful than the shiny ones.

When the distance between them became short, Agnus stepped to the side of the path and waited. The floppy passed first. As he did, the tail ceased its perpetual motion, and the eyes became fixed on his friend. The floppy knew him! A little jealousy sprang up with the thought that maybe the two of them were friends. But that would be good, he decided! These thoughts vanished as the other two approached. They still loudly talked and laughed as they passed by. It was strange! There was no greeting or recognition at all. Not even a look was exchanged! They did not know that he was in their presence. They must have been totally wrapped up in their own thoughts and plans to have not seen!

Agnus stepped back upon the trail and continued his journey. Adam stood up so as to get a longer view of the disappearing figure and was about to give a whistle to say good-bye when he realized he had not done a really smart thing. The two legs had seen his motion and were now very excited. Even as the shiny sticks were being raised, Adam gave a final look in all directions. It was beautiful! Even at the end of the cooling period, it was beautiful! As he entered, he heard tiny thuds everywhere, and tiny bits of dirt and rock were flung into his home. Then there were two loud noises. Adam knew that last look was almost extremely costly—but well worth it, he thought! The hunters of the long ears would not let an opportunity like him go by.

As Adam plodded deeper toward his sleep chamber and safety, for the first time he became aware that his right paw did not complain, and even his dampness-diseased hips were of no discomfort. He was puzzled at this. He

Ron L. Kuntz

was also happy and did not dwell on why he felt so good. Perhaps the pain would return if he thought long on it.

Arriving at the well-lined chamber, Adam suddenly became very sleepy indeed. It was now an overpowering sensation. There was that mighty, gaping yawn, a final stretch, and he curled up in as tight a ball as he could with the now scrawny tail covering his nose. He never looked forward to the sleep periods. He knew they were necessary, but he was reminded too much of the departure. Agnus had said that he would return to see him again when his sleep was done. He promised! That thought made him very happy. That promise brought a smile. He had felt this way many cycles ago as he cuddled against Mother. It was good to feel this way again. Adam smiled very contentedly!

The floppy had been brought to the entrance and, as any scent-curious floppy would do, plunged his blunt nose in as deeply as possible. Whistle-pig burrows were always of interest! As the sensation of this scent was sorted and analyzed by the floppy's brain, a plan of action was quickly decided upon. Memories returned! It was best to quickly pull the delicate nose out of *this* burrow and to continue to try to find a long ear to chase. The masters were not amused by this action and gave a boot to the rump of the poor floppy as he began his retreat.

Curled up in a ball and knowing he was safe, Adam listened to the sounds that echoed down to his laid back ears. There came muffled sniffs, angry words, a thump, a yelp, and then laughter. It was not the laughter that his new friend would ever use. He really liked that floppy, and his mind began to darken at the sounds. They were not nice two legs! The words Agnus had told him came back to him, and the dark thoughts vanished. Happiness and serenity reigned once again. A fleeting thought of the nicely scented female brought a smile and two feeble tail thumps. The floppy was happy again! The scent of a long ear had been found, and the joyous, drawn-out howls meant the trail was warm. This was good. The floppy was happy, and he could never match the swiftness of the long ear.

Adam knew that he should get up and seal the entrance against the coming bitter cold, but he was tired, and the urge to sleep was strong. He told himself that the sealing of the entrance could wait until his nap was over. He knew this was not true! He was aware that his heart and breathing had already started to slow down. It was happening so fast this time! His slowing mind wondered. Was it his age? Or was it his happiness? The questions did not linger, for soon he was asleep. The sleep deepened as his heart and breathing were again slowing to a mimicking of the departure. The two loud, sharp noises on the surface went unheard.

So he slept. The dark orb had grown full twice and almost to the third time. How fast did it pass? Time has no meaning to the dead or to those who pretend it. As the dark orb reached its third fullness, Adam's heart began to beat a little faster. It went over five beats a minute and then faster and faster. The blood coursed more quickly through his whistle-pig brain. His breathing increased in perfect proportion to his heartbeat. The brain began to function again. At last he was able to dream. It was a simple yet wonderful dream. He had turned a corner and had seen the light as he had done as a pup.

Ron L. Kuntz

His nose was now able to twitch, and twitch it did! The light was soft and far away. As it was years before, he had to reach it, and a new world would open to him. This time he did not blink. He knew that he must go to that light. The tired legs began to move. It was so hard at first! It was much harder than it was fighting gravity for the first time. The small paws began to move faster and faster, and in the need and the excitement, his tail began to thump faster and faster. The light grew brighter and closer as the paws and tail moved at a frantic pace. When at last he reached the light, the now gray, scrawny tail became quiet, and the tiny legs ceased their movement.

The Agnus had kept his promise.

Adam was happy! Very, very happy!

About the Author

Ron was raised in the country and grew to know the wild animals in their natural habitat. He still lives less than a mile from his childhood home. He received degrees in chemistry and geology and taught the sciences for thirty years.

Ron married his princess in 1968 and has tried to enjoy all the time spent on this wondrous planet of God's!